# Internet Interactive
# Teacher's Key -Dead Men

# Dwarf at Winsor Ruins

Product Utility

Critical Thinking

Knowledge Comprehension

Application Analysis Synthesis

And EVALUATION.

Available At Trafford publishing.com./ Also In E Book

Executive Editor\ Education Specialist: Dr. Jamie L Lial

STUDENTS STARR TEST STUDY DIRECTORY LINKS ENGLISH

AND SPANISH

Grades 4 to 11th

MADE IN USA

President Barack Obama

"As we began the 21st century, education
is first. For no child to be left behind
is .paramount, head start to college. Step up."

Trafford
PUBLISHING®  www.trafford.com
North America & international
toll-free: 844-688-6899 (USA & Canada)
fax: 812 355 4082

**mac**

mississippi arts commission
inspire enrich

RE:    Mississippi Arts Commission – Teaching Artist Roster Directory

Dear Parker Chamberlain:

Congratulations on the success you are having in writing about Mississippi from a historic perspective. The landscapes/places you mentioned are all very interesting.

As requested, I am enclosing a copy of the guidelines and application form and other pertinent information for the Teaching Artist Roster. I am also including the information for the Fellowship opportunity, but as we have already discussed this opportunity is for in-state artists. The arts education program director is Kim Whitt and her contact information is: (601) 359-6037 – kwhitt@arts.state.ms.us

If I can provide you with additional information, please don't hesitate to contact me.

Sincerely,

Diane Williams
Arts Industry Program Director & Accessibility Coordinator

/dw
Enclosures

Quotes: 1 OF 5. VENESSA P CHAMBERLAIN REMEMBER TO ANSWER THE TESTS YOU MUST READ THE INTERNET INTERACTIVE STUDENT READER OF THE LAGEND OF DEAD MAN DWARF AT WINSOR RUINS/ AND THE LEGEND OF BLUE WATER TREASURE EPISODES 1 THRU 5. HAPPY READING

THE LEGEND OF

DEAD MEN DWARF
AT WINSOR RUINS

and the Legend of Blue Water Treasure

PARKER CHAMBERLAIN

Teacher's Key

Internet/Interactive

Skills & Use

Test/ Activities

Test for: Deadmen Dwarf At Winsor Ruins: Reader

Test for: Bluewater Treasure at Winsor Ruins: Reader.

**Product Utility**
**Critical Thinking**
**Knowledge Comprehension**
**Application Analysis Synthesis**
**And EVALUATION.**
**Available At Trafford publishing.com./ Also In E Book**

Published by:    Trafford Publishing
Blooming, IN.
W.TraffordPublishing.com
Reign of the 44th 2011

First Edition:
Grade Use 4th - 12th

Author: Parker Chamberlain
Illustrator: Parker Chamberlain
Editor: Dr. Jamie Lail

Teacher's Key

Deadmen Dwarf at Winsor Ruins

Bluewater Treasure at Winsor Ruins

Internet: Interactive:   Work Lab: Key
                         Cyberskills and Use
                         Interactive Web Classroom Activities

Program Author:     Parker Chamberlain
Editor:             Adejoke Oresanya
Executive Editor:   Dr. Jamie Lail
Book Illustrator:   Parker Chamberlain

Publication# 001

ISBN:

Copyright January 1, 2011

Parker Chamberlain

Grand Prairie, Texas

**EMERALD MOUND**

You are invited to the top

Before you is the second largest temple mound in the United States. Only Monks Mound in Cahokia, Illinois, is larger. This eight acre mound, constructed from a natural hill, was built and used from about 1300 to 1600 by the Mississippians, ancestors of the Natchez Indians.

Unlike dome shaped mounds constructed only for burials, Emerald Mound supported temples, ceremonial structures, and burials of a complex society's civic and religious leaders.

UNITED STATES DEPARTMENT OF THE INTERIOR
NATIONAL PARK SERVICE

**Pontatoc**

# Deadmen Dwarf At Winsor Ruins
## Work Book Key

Questions: 1 thought 240

Answers:

1. Mississippi
2. Clabourne
3. Cigarette / Ill placed
4. Claborne County Mississippi
5. A war between Northern states and Southern states in the United States, a class war of human rights
6. Religious meeting/ church
7. Spider /Black Widow / Extremely Poisonous
8. Black Fang(very large intelligent bat)
9. Poisonous bite
10. Razor, eavesdropping to protect Chicha from him
11. A tree(Africanus Dwarf)
12. In Big Red (Barn, front corner stall)
13. A barn
14. Mother Razor, wife of Big Skeezzer
15. An Egyptian Cobra
16. A river, tributary of the Mississippi
17. Amite
18. Royal Female Pig

19. Blue Mule
20. Widow
21. Gloster
22. State Representative
23. Royal Black Crow
24. Chewing Tobacco
25. Subversion, Oppression
26. Three
27. Magpie(bird)
28. Smith Daniel Coffee
29. Crop Inspector
30. McCormick Heater
31. No free blacks in Mississippi, Jim Crow Law, Reinforcement
32. Uncle Guy
33. Widow
34. Egyptian Black Cobra
35. Pork Skin
36. Philosophical, Organization of Free Mason (singular answer) down line order of King Solomon
37. At 4 poplars, on the south forty acres of Winsor plantation.

# Deadmen Dwarf At Winsor Ruins
## Work Book Key

38. Husband of Julia Chamberlain-lawmaker and brother-in-law of Parker Chamberlain in the story.

39. David and Julia Green.

40. Teacher

41. Sister to Parker Chamberlain, David Green's wife.

42. Sister

43. Hints

44. A guide to find objects.

45. Rare obtainable, objects (A through E)

46. 2,600

47. New England

48. Roman

49. 1871

50. Mississippi legislature

51. Whigs/ Unionist

52. 1851

53. Three

54. 1840

55. Presbyterian

56. 250 acres

57. The chapel

58. Port Gibson

59.  A breed of dog
60.  A Big Red
61.  3
62.  Crystallized salt
63.  Directional findings (GPS)
64.  Whiskey, Corn liquor; Moon shine
65.  Black magic powder
66.  Holy Water
67.  A tributary river to the Mississippi river
68.  Burial place
69.  No order
70.  Sap
71.  Frightened
72.  Bible
73.  Shock, fright
74.  Loon
75.  Loon
76.  Black Fang
77.  Winkey and gang
78.  Yes
79.  Owl(great horned)
80.  Mississippi

# Deadmen Dwarf At Winsor Ruins
## Work Book Key

81. Winkey

82. $175,000(3.5million today)

83. Wife of Smith Daniel Coffee (and cousin), owner of Winsor Plantation

84. North of Port Gibson, 1/2 mile

85. Clabourne

86. Attic

87. 2

88. 3

89. Supporting the roof of the house

90. In Mississippi at Winsor ruins

91. An agency for historic sites, preservation

92. A possum

93. A nose

94. Dead Bon Jim

95. The blinding by Tree at Winkey and Old Mann

96. Herring fish, salted and canned

97. 6 per tin can

98. He died

99. A beanie (copter cap)

100. A. Contractor editor B. Word processor

101. Author Parker Chamberlain

102. An Indian burial mound

103. A Choctaw, mystic, Medicine Man

104. Choctaw?

105. A royal crow(bird)

106. Epiphany / his sister

107. A royal male crow and Howie's cousin

108. A royal female crow, Howie's cousin

109. A royal female crow, Howie's cousin

110. A royal male crow, Howie's cousin

111. Me Donald's dumpster

112. A witch's spell

113. Ana banks, a nickname for Loon in Deadmen Dwarf

114. An African American female, 9 years old

115. Nose of a critter, possum, pig, etc.

116. A royal crown male

117. A female English pig

118. In Big Red, the barn on Tome Hawk Farms

119. Widow

120. Black Fang

121. A Magpie

122. Red Fox

123. Rosetta Fox

124. Senora
125. A murder of crows
126. Yellow belly chickens
127. Fox Tail
128. 100
129. Howie's great grandparent (A political representative, symbol of subversion and oppression)
130. A deceptive action
131. A royal crow
132. Subversion
133. In Tomahawk Farms and surrounding farm communities of Black Fang
134. In the mind of man/ Tomahawk Farm Community of Creatures
135. Social politics use people against each other. Brother against brother, sister against sister, to the death by any and all means.

136. A social political mind virus utilizes the cybernetic super highway to time travel. From generation to generation, Jim Crow travels by whisper, also mind to mind. It can only be forgotten, immobilized, or anesthetized, but never killed. Jim Crow is immortal.

137. Put to sleep! Immobilized! Forgotten!

138. Cybernetics, Mind to Mind, Social Politics, Time Jumper

139. A royal crow (male)

Internet Activity Research:

140. Constant observation by the watch birds and other subversive, critter tactics employing subjugation, and in some cases death, as with Widow and Razor.

    A. Define    B. Define
    A. Forced economics submission
    B. Forced economic responsibility

Internet Research Political Aspect Question:

141. Oppression, subjugation (?)

142. Spy birds, always one-step ahead of everyone and non-participating With the common critters. Always aloof, <u>hides in plain sight</u>, inducing fear of speaking out

143. Fear of death for their loved ones and themselves.

144. Nite/Night

145. Howie Crow-great great grandparent

146. The death of two slaves and the hiding of Winsor treasure; the use of subversion and oppression to control people using witch craft as a tool.

147. Lord Winsor and two slaves

148. Naga Eina

149. Big Skeezer

150. Five owls

151. Fear; mobbing attempt; public bullying

152. The feed bin

153. Crash mobbed into Emerald Cloud's Pond

154. Emerald Cloud

155. Crashed into the watering pond

156. The warm, smiling face of Emerald Cloud

157. An owl war party, chaired by Big Hoots

158. Public execution; enforced subversion and oppression under the threat of death; terror tactics

159. Gathered around the feed bin, crying as she slipped away.

160. Chicha

161. Jim Crow

162. Their lives and children's future are at stake.

163. Lord Winsor

164. You would not recognize his in the present or future and none of your children's future generation would know of his tactics; blindsided.

165. Immortal, mind traveler, generation to generation.

166. The sea of minds. Cybernetic Super Highway.

167. Chicha

168. Killed Razor

169. Black Fang

170. Widow's boss (Black Raven)

171. The Ravens

172. Passed out at the sight of Red Beast, stuffed possum.

173. Boot; shirt

174. Slave driver, enforcer.

175. A bird, (magpie)

176. A persimmon tree

177. Drinking rock

178. Big Hoots crash into Miss Daisy
179. Little Hoots
180. Osolot Cat
181. Airport Culvert
182. Gorilla tactics
183. "The blessed bring chaos to order through divine prayer."
184. 11 year old Will Bank; brother of Loon and Old Man
185. Cousin of Bradear and Nasa.
186. A great horned owl
187. Black Fang
188. Black Fang
189. His mother was injured falling into the cave
190. Poncho's dead mother
191. Black Fang's family of 2 million bats
192. Black Fang
193. 6 inch sharp bat fangs
194. Split personalities in one being
195. Black Fang
196. Poncho
197. Poncho Fox
198. Poncho Fox

199. An Egyptian Cobra, Female, 20ft long, 200lbs, dangerous
200. An Egyptian Cobra, Female, 20ft long, 200lbs, dangerous
201. Cobra, pit viper
202. A blue mule; representing Parker Chamberlain (Great Uncle Tom Coffee)
203. One hundred eleven
204. Chicha
205. 111 is a deer (name) Anna Green
206. Big Tom
207. A possum
208. Black Fang

*Bonus Question-Barack Obama

209. Excessive noise

## Deadmen Dwarf At Winsor Ruins
## Work Book Key

(1-Net) Research question Activities for the Internet:

210. Abdomen

211. River Boat (Show Boat). Stream driven, single pusher peddles

212. Mississippi Queen, Sprague, Delta Queen

213. Mississippi

214. Self destruction

215. Big Hoots

216. 1-Net Class Activity: A,B,C,D,E,F, group activity will yield multiple answers, discussion, to analyze which answer are correct. 3 page essays.

217. Paddle Wheel, Delta Queen, Mississippi Queen

218. A political idea that lives in the sea of minds from generation to generation. Similar to racism.

219. Subversion, oppression, fear, terrorism, death

220. An author (express the details of his work)

221. An author

222. Bre Dear

223. Mark Twain

224. 1871

225. Mississippi

226. Mississippi

# Deadmen Dwarf At Winsor Ruins
## Work Book Key

Test Lab Research · Questions:

227. Research Jim Crow politics and its structured mechanics (how it works). 5 page essay.

228. Define: How Jim Crow was applied in Legend of Blue Water by page and line number.

229. Group Discussion: Locate page and line demonstrating the aggressiveness of Jim Crow politics.

230. Locate line and page for oppression and how it is applied.

231. Group Discussion: Elimination; its effect on the oppressed. Log Answers, Black Board Analysis or Desktop.

232. Adolf Hitler and his application of Nazi politics and the similarities to Jim Crow. 5 page essay.

233. White paper essay (5 pages) comparison of Joseph Stalin's politics to Jim Crpw. Note the similarities and differences.

Internet Activity: Test Lab

234. Define how President Barack Obama encounter Jim –Crow politics during his presidency "!" a lame duck congress and senate.

235. 5 page essay comparison defining the differences between "lame duck presidency" and Jim Crow politics.

236. Define how Jim Crow politics affected the United States and list during Barack Obama's presidency and list how it may have been applied to create and contribute to the 9% unemployment rate (highest of the time). What could be implemented to disrupt this type of oppression? Describe your solution (10 page essay).

237. Define: Answer: Travels in the sea of human minds, generation to generation, through transmigration ideas, whisper, social networking. Nazism, Marxist, Zouism, Ho-Chi-Min, etc.

238. Always recognize your enemy; learn his "modus operandi" tools, he uses (Fear, shock, mass anger, terrorism, death).

239. How can Jim Crow politics be eliminated from American and worldwide politics? (Suggestion: Open answer question. Allow the student to answer and select the best three through class vote).
    Answer: _____

240. A. What is emerald mound? An Indian burial mound for the Natchez Indians.
    B. Where is Emerald Mound located? Adam County, Mississippi.
    C. Who did Emerald Cloud save from his pond? Little Red.
    D. Who is Emerald Cloud? Chickasaw Elder
    E. Elder Shaman/ Medicine man

## Internet

Group Activities: Research, other burial mounds. Discuss the purpose, designs throughout the world, include great pyramids of Egypt

Collect: 5 page essay about this burial system, grade on contents, detail, assembly and comprehension.

The research continues: visit Trafford. com for more of the author Parker Chamberlain.

*Disclaimer: Parker Chamberlain*

*As with all education products, the author created this product as training system for simple assessments of reading, writing entertainment its educational value is ascertained by the user of this product*

*Author: Parker Chamberlain*
*Illustrations: Parker Chamberlain*
*Copyrights:]anuary1, 2012 All rights reserved.*
*Parker Chamberlain*

# Great New Reads By:

# Parker Chamberlain

Ava Now: Dead Men Dwarf at Winsor Ruins

Coming Attraction's Cover Pages for Website

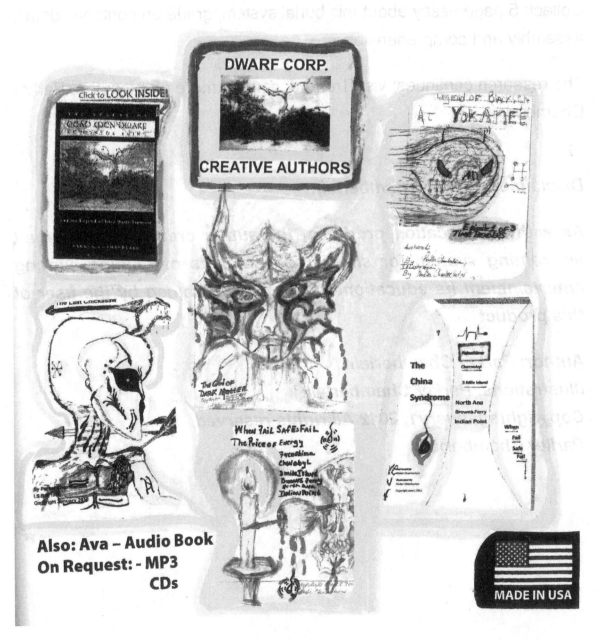

Our stories continue:   All titles below are available in EBook

Order your copies at TraffordPublishing.com. Author search: Parker Chamberlain

1.   Deadmen Dwarf at Winsor Ruins:        Episodes 1-4. Includes:
         ISBN: 1466945923                          Teacher's Edition and Key,
                                                   Interactive, Student Workbook.

2.   The Last Chickasaw                     Episodes 1-7
3.   The Legend of Pali Goddess             Episodes -1-6
     of Fire
4.   The China Syndrome: When Fail          Episodes 1-3
     Safes Fail Fucushima Diechi,
     Chonabyl, 3- Mile Island
5.   The God of Dark Matter                 Episodes 1-3
6.   The Legend of the Aquanista's          Episodes 1-3
     at Bakini Atoll
7.   Chief Firebull's Last Stand at         Episodes 1-3
     Fort Hill
8.   Spirit Walkers and Blood Drop          Episodes 1-3
9.   Pontatoc Captures the Skin             Episodes 1-3
     Walkers
10.  Pontatoc and Blood Drop: The           Episodes 1-3
     Capture of an Indian Princess
11.  Emerald Cloud and the Mast of          Episodes 1-3
     the Spirit Walkers
12.  The Legend of Black Lightening
     at Yakanee

All products developed by Parker Chamberlain:

1. Books with 42 episodes/2004
2. Teacher's Edition /2014
3. Student Lab/ Online Immersion

4. Teacher's Key/ Online Analysis
5. Story Stix
6. EBooks
7. Audio Books
8. Music CDs The Legend of Deadmen Dwarf at Windsor Ruins Music Google/Amazon
9. YouTube Trailer and video

Engage in the mystical world of short stories by Parker Chamberlain. Get a free Amazon Nook with proof of purchase shown for every story in the series. Mail purchase receipts and barcodes to:

P.O. Box 530246
Grand Prairie, TX 75050

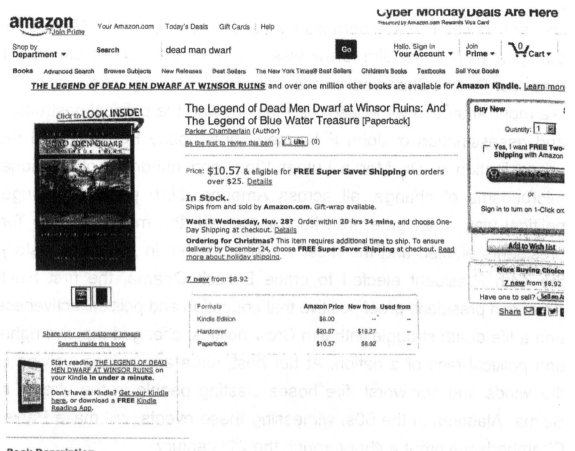

**amazon**
Join Prime

Your Amazon.com   Today's Deals   Gift Cards   Help

Shop by Department ▾    Search    dead man dwarf    Go    Hello. Sign in Your Account ▾    Join Prime ▾    Cart ▾

Books   Advanced Search   Browse Subjects   New Releases   Best Sellers   The New York Times® Best Sellers   Children's Books   Textbooks   Sell Your Books

**THE LEGEND OF DEAD MEN DWARF AT WINSOR RUINS** and over one million other books are available for **Amazon Kindle.** Learn more

Click to LOOK INSIDE!

## The Legend of Dead Men Dwarf at Winsor Ruins: And The Legend of Blue Water Treasure [Paperback]
Parker Chamberlain (Author)

Be the first to review this item | Like (0)

Price: **$10.57** & eligible for **FREE Super Saver Shipping** on orders over $25. Details

**In Stock.**
Ships from and sold by **Amazon.com**. Gift-wrap available.

**Want it Wednesday, Nov. 28?** Order within 20 hrs 34 mins, and choose One-Day Shipping at checkout. Details

**Ordering for Christmas?** This item requires additional time to ship. To ensure delivery by December 24, choose **FREE Super Saver Shipping** at checkout. Read more about holiday shipping.

**7 new** from $8.92

| Formats | Amazon Price | New from | Used from |
|---|---|---|---|
| Kindle Edition | $8.00 | -- | -- |
| Hardcover | $20.57 | $18.27 | -- |
| Paperback | $10.57 | $8.92 | -- |

Share your own customer images
Search inside this book

Start reading THE LEGEND OF DEAD MEN DWARF AT WINSOR RUINS on your Kindle **in under a minute.**

Don't have a Kindle? Get your Kindle here, or download a **FREE** Kindle Reading App.

**Buy New**

Quantity: 1

☐ Yes, I want FREE Two-Shipping with Amazon

Add to Cart

or

Sign in to turn on 1-Click ord

Add to Wish List

**More Buying Choice**
**7 new** from $8.92
Have one to sell? Sell on A

Share ✉ 📘 🐦

## Book Description
Publication Date: **September 25, 2012**

Parker Chamberlain; brings to his readers every Childs Secret wish, a treasure hunt set to a historical background of southern plantations; lege the oldest Plantation in Mississippi Winsor Ruins; this story has the flavor of Mark Twain's Huckel Berry Finn; a drop of Edgar Allen Poe's Darkne Fiction. Parker Chamberlain in his author's word utilized Julia and David green a living examples that down line slave descendents have obtaine unique place in American Politics and the communities in the state of Mississippi. The honorable David Green was elected to the office of State Representative for District 96 and is a graduate of Al Corn State University, this university was established by the Mississippi Legislature in 187 first graduate from this university as a down line slave descendant to be elected to public office to service the community as from the very legi: body that chartered the first and largest black university in the history of the state of Mississippi since the civil war, this has never been possibl the 1963 and 1964 voting rights act was approved by John F. Kennedy and the congress of the united stated; these leaps and bounds, in socia political change that began with the emancipation proclamation form the 1800's thru the 1900's, brought political change and self realization to Negros, that education was not just a dream, but a doorway that accessed the stair well to power in America; a clear message Unlocked by Pre

⤓Show More

## Special Offers and Product Promotions
- **Giving this item as a gift?** If Amazon.com is the seller, we can wrap it for you for the special price of $2.99. Just choose the gift-wrap op when available at checkout, and let Amazon.com help make your holiday season hassle-free.

## Product Details
**Paperback:** 68 pages
**Publisher:** Trafford (September 25, 2012)
**Language:** English
**ISBN-10:** 1466945923
**ISBN-13:** 978-1466945920
**Product Dimensions:** 6 x 0.2 x 9 inches
**Shipping Weight:** 5.4 ounces (View shipping rates and policies)
**Average Customer Review:** Be the first to review this item

# About the Author

Parker Chamberlain was born during the late 50's in Fayette, Mississippi, during a time when Jim Crow was the most dangerous criminal in America; Parker Chamberlain is a, native of Vicksburg, Mississippi. He like most American witnessed the Vietnam war, the political destruction and assassination of John F Kennedy and Bobby Kennedy and the assassination of Dr. Martin Luther King, and hundreds of individual microcosms of change, all across America, birth pains of change, political war, water gate. Iran kuntra scandal, the moon landing. Ten presidents elected and the most surprising event in American history, the 44th President elected to office Barack Obama, the first black American president, proof positive that education and political activeness and a life death struggle with Jim Crow politics, changed the civil rights and political face of a nation. At her best, stars and stripes waiving in the winds and her worst, fire hoses blasting people in the streets in Selma, Alabama in the 60s, witnessing these events, will make Parker Chamberlain a great author through the 21st century.

# Getting Into The Flow:

Author: Parker Chamberlain

We Hope You Enjoyed Dead Men's Dwarf at Winsor Ruins!

"On The Road Home"

Coffey/Coffie Family Reunion
July 2010 -Fayette /Natchez, Mississippi

The story of West James and Julia coffee James was lived out in this intrepid plantation house as you look at this picture it is a reminder that our lives and life works are finite, as you look at this picture you don't see the years of barbe Q's, parties. Planting green gardens, picking tomatoes beans corn, okra, hide -n-go seek games we played happy and sad times. Those moments are compressed into our minds, the grand children of this couple. My grand children will only see this broken down rusting weathered hulk of a house in this book because time has erased this home but the families that were born in this home are flourishing scattered around America, Milton L. James and Shelly James. and Hester James Chamberlain are the down line slave descendants of the this family, that has produced Teachers, Doctors Lawyers, Dentist, politicians, and many others, because of REAL TREASURE, EDUCATION, OUR PARENTS, STEPPED UP, AND REMINDED THEIR CHILDREN, NEVER FORGET JIM CROW IS IMMORTAL, AND PREYS ON IGNORANCE.

Bibliography of Julia Green

Julia Chamberlain Greene/graduate of Alcorn State University Magna Cum Laude, Master Degree in education minor in Biology, scientist, teacher at Gloster High Gloster, Mississippi, political actvists co. Campaign Manager for the honorable David Green, Eastern Starr Prince Hall, Alpha Kappa Alpha Sara, Avid Democrat, Southern Baptist. 1947 to 1995, Transcended.

**Dead Men Dwarf**
**Folklore Art & Illustrations**
**By**
**Author Parker Chamberlain**

# The Last Chickasaw

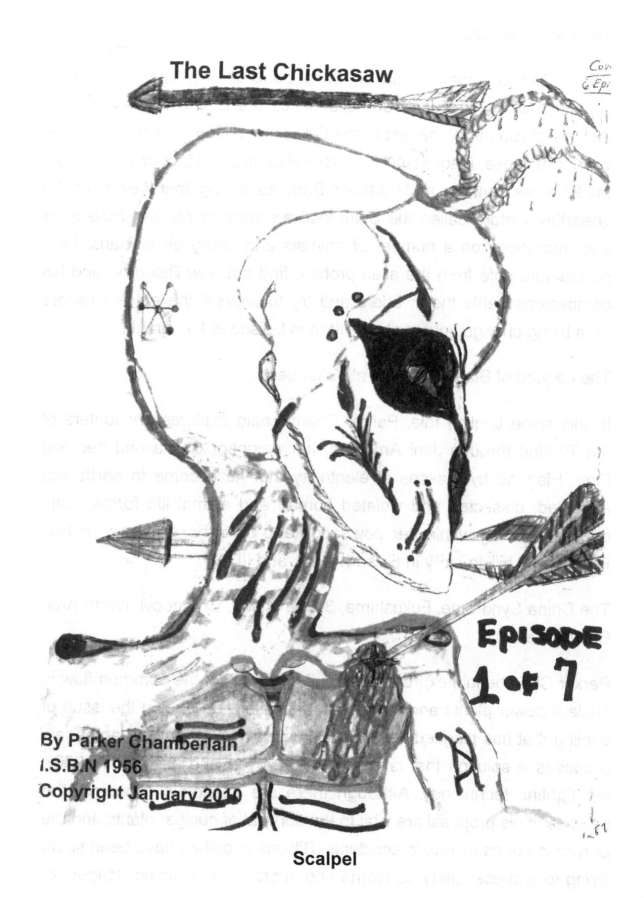

**EPISODE 1 OF 7**

**By Parker Chamberlain**
**I.S.B.N 1956**
**Copyright January 2010**

**Scalpel**

The Last Chikasaw:

Author Parker Chamberlain brings a bone-chilling tale of a Native American close encounter of the 6th kind. 'the Last Chikasaw" follows the tale of Bloodrop, the last of the Chikasaw nation, and his sister, the warrior princess, Isaqueena. The story also involves Bloodrop's captive, the Princess Pontatoc and his friend Bremstone. Together they battle the unearthly visitors called the Spirit Walkers performing live dissections and mutilations on a number of animals and finally on humans. With no creature safe from the alien probes, find out how Bloodrop and his companions battle the invaders and try to prevent the entire villagers from being changed overnight. Written in Episodes I, II, and III.

The Legend of Black Lightning at Yokanee:

In this spine tingling tale, Parker Chamberlain explores encounters of the 7th kind through Jani Ambroso, her neighbor Salina and her dog Ping. Plagued by masses of electricity that have come to earth and abducted, dissected and violated human and animal life forms, Jami does everything within her power to keep safe those closest to her. Follow this chilling story in Episodes I, II, and III.

The China Syndrome: Fukushima, 3 Mile Island, Chernobyl, North Ana, Browns Ferry:

Parker Chamberlain expresses an authorial view of the common flaw in nuclear power plants and an educated solution. Regarding the issue of cooling that has plagued the plant industry since its birth, Chamberlain proposes a solution that is simple and proven and as old as 1980's fire fighting technology. Although there are economic concerns, the benefits of his proposal are vital to the survival of nuclear plants and the prevention of catastrophic accidents. Billions of dollars have been spent trying to address safety concerns and improve the looming dangers of the industry. Chamberlain exposes a way that would be cost effective, efficient, and above everything else, successful. Revealed in Episodes I, II, and III, Chamberlain tackles the "giant elephant in the corner" head on through a compelling and intelligent documentary.

# The Last Chickasaw

**Pontatoc**

# Folklore Art

**I am Razor**

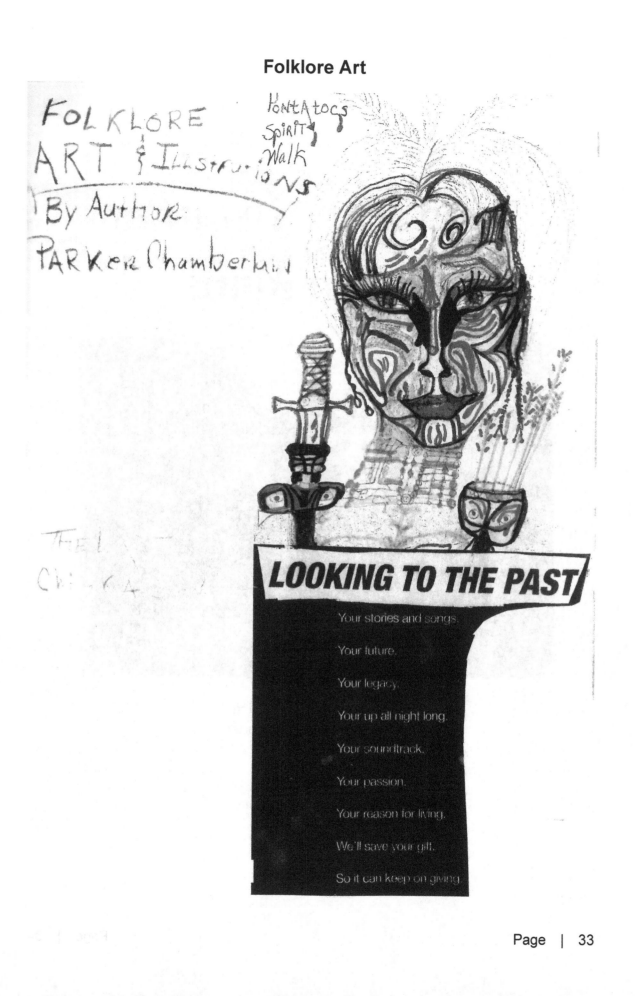

# Dead Men  Dwarf at Winsor Ruins

Author Parker Chamberlain
Illustrator Parker Chamberlain

I displayed

Dwarf Dancing: this form of celebration was performed by slaves that had escaped from below the Mason Dixon Line to Freedom from slavery. It has many different names. Other names are Gig Dancing, Hippie Hop, Gigie Gig, Hopping Bodily, Slapp Happy and Black Gal. all of these folklore nicknames for dancing to the joy of escaping slavery oppression to freedom – wherever you found

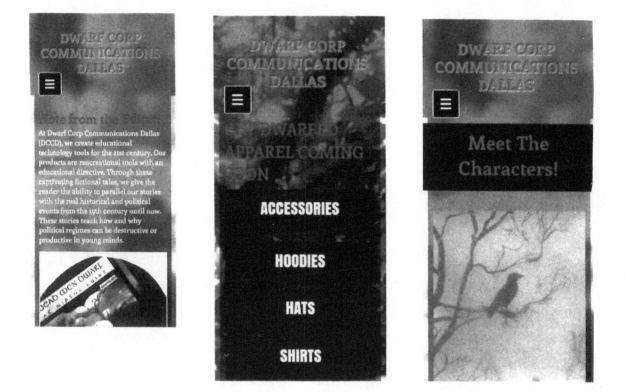

Audio (original motion picture sound track)

This is a compilation of music combined with the story telling of the Legend of the Dead Men at Winsor Ruins, chapter by chapter to improve the readers immersion in the suspense of the story and its powerful cliff hanger and beauty of reader and movie enjoyment to enhance the reader's excitement and spine-tingling experience of this well-woven story.

# Folklore Music G6

New Sound Track G6

This sound track is a compilation of exciting lyrics, designed for pure enjoyment as the young people of today and future readers may call it twerking music and spirit swelling harmonious tunes to bring joy to listeners, immersion in the movie and readers enjoyment of the story. Dance your ears off to G6 and its powerful spirit lifting tunes and lyrics.

# You can order Deadmen Dwarf logoed travel apparel

BACK VIEW

BLACK/BLACK   DARK CHARCOAL/   ROYAL/BLACK   CHILI RED/BLACK
BLACK

**NEW!**
**SPORT-TEK®**
**FLEXFIT® AIR**
**MESH BACK CAP**
**STC40** $11.98
ADULT SIZES: S/M, L/XL

MOISTURE-
WICKING

| FABRIC | 83/14/3 nylon/cotton/ spandex front panels; 87/13 poly/spandex air mesh mid and back panels |
|---|---|
| STRUCTURE | Structured |
| PROFILE | Mid |
| CLOSURE | Stretch fit |

**STC40**

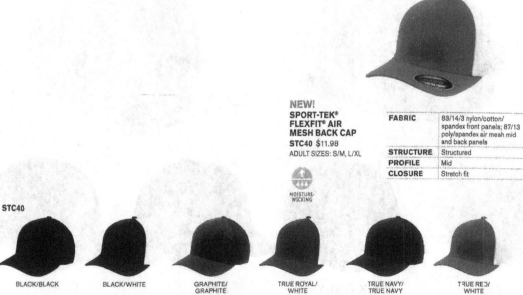

BLACK/BLACK   BLACK/WHITE   GRAPHITE/   TRUE ROYAL/   TRUE NAVY/   TRUE RED/
GRAPHITE   WHITE   TRUE NAVY   WHITE

# Request these items with email address
# and phone. dwarfcorp@aol.com

You can order Dead Men Dwarf logoed travel apparel

**NEW**
**PORT! NEW!**
**PORT PORT AUTHORITY® FLEXFIT® DELTA®**
**ICAP ⊃ CAP C938 $26.00**
ALDULT ADULT SIZES: S/M, L/XL

| | | |
|---|---|---|
| FABRJL **FABRIC** | 92/8 poly/spandex; 100% polyester undervisor |
| STRUC **STRUCTURE** | Structured |
| PROF **PROFILE** | Mid |
| FEAEJC **FEATURES** | Seam-sealed, quick-drying, 3-layer sweatband with stain-blocking technology<br>4 die-cut vent eyelets |
| OSU **CLOSURE** | Stretch fit |

SILVER          DARK GREY          NAVY          BLACK

Request these items with email address
and phone. dwarfcorp@aol.com

# NEW!
## PORT AUTHORITY® FORM BACKPACK
**BG212 $57.00**

This structured, protective backpack is sleek and modern—perfect for today's commuter or businessperson.

- Strategic top pocket with EVA-molded lid to protect phone, sunglasses or valuables
- Side-entry dedicated padded laptop zippered pocket
- Padded main compartment with zippered mesh pocket on back panel
- Zippered front compartment with padded tablet sleeve, organizer pockets and elastic accessories holders
- Zoned spacer mesh padded back
- Adjustable slide sternum strap
- Side stretch-mesh beverage pockets
- Padded spacer mesh shoulder straps with built-in grab handle

| DIMENSIONS | Laptop sleeve dimensions: 9.25"h x 9.5"w; fits most 15" laptops<br>Dimensions: 19"h x 11.5"w x 6.5"d; Approx. 1,420 cubic inches |
|---|---|
| MATERIALS | 1,680 denier ballistic polyester |

Other products and logos:

See our logos for caps, hats and t-shirts, sweat shirt, back pack, hoodies, nap sacks. Use the price list and logo collection to select a custom fit for your exciting reader flare.

BACK VIEW

BLACK          DARK GREY/BLACK

**BG212 $57.00**

Request these items with email address
and phone. dwarfcorp@aol.com

## Folklore Art

I Got Dwarfed, Get Dwarfed, Sexy Dwarf, reading dwarf apparel. See our apparel catalogue on line at:

I'm Dwarfed, Dead Men Dwarf, Get Dwarfed, Got Dwarfed, Hot Dwarf, Sexy Dwarf, Smart Dwarf, Genius Dwarf, Dead Men Gold, Dead Bone Jim, Happy Dwarf, Dwarf Homie – all for you as fans of The Legend of Dead Men Dwarf at Winsor Ruins.

Request these logos with your email, payment and phone. dwarfcorp@aol.com

Customize your reader coolness with many other cool logos by author Parker Chamberlain for the Last Chikasaw, A Very Cool Alien Close Encounter of the 4th and the 5th kind with a spine-tingling logo of Nest Leaders Scalpel or Razor and all of the Human & Nest Gangsters, Skinners. Add a logo that defines your reader skills with these great spine-tingling, Goosebumpers, Mind bernder stories. Enjoy your hats, caps and t-shirt, hoodies and back packs on the apparel website:

DwarfCorpcommunication.com Order 24/7 your custom apparel on our shopping site:

Please an order request on Dwarfcorp@aol.com

Visa/Master Card/ American Express or check card.

Allow 3 to 6 weeks for delivery of your cool logo items.

Check out our music and get Zombified or a Zombie logo by special order on the site:

Dwarfcorp@gmail.com Specify cap size only and color. Limited Quantity: 1 per client

Thanks for your support: Movie Fund Investment Program. (link)

See our Gofundme/gwnm3s and enjoy our movie production site development funding plan

# Screenshot of Folklore Storytelling

Screenshot of Folklore Storytelling

# The Legend of Black Lightning at Yok-a-nee

**Episode 1 of 3**

**Time Benders**

Authored by:

Parker Chamberlain

Illustrated by:

Parker Chamberlain

The beginning of Black Lightning at Yok-a-nee

I was talking to my son about growing up in Vicksburg, Mississippi and he asked if I had ever heard of any adventure stories. I sad, "Well, my Great Uncle, actually, my Great Uncle George Wolf, and I were replacing the rook to this old man's house. I was nine years old, full of spitfire and loved a good story. I was hauling the old shingles in a wheelbarrow and dumping them in the bed of the pickup. As I hauled them the old man told me a story.

He said, "This your first time in the Yakanee?' I said 'No sir. We pass this way every other weekend on our way to my Grandma's farm in Fayette. We look after her farm. He smiled a snaggle-tooth smile, drew in a breath and said, "That is Yokanee. It is my tribal name.' I replied, 'Wow, are you a real American Indian?' he laughed out said and said, 'Brother George! Old Bredear wants to know if I am a real Injun!' my uncle also laughed and said, 'Bredear, he is the worst kind. Educated and broke.' They both rolled with laughter. After they calmed down, I said this place was off the map and as back woods as I had ever seen. Mana Wak looked at me very seriously and said, 'If you get lost in these woods and sticks, the Legend of Yakanee's blue and black lightening will find you. The name is Black Lightening and by the time you see them... "Bang, Bang" my friend. You are done.'

I turned to my uncle as if to ask if that was true. Mana Wak spoke in a whisper, 'It is getting dark. Stay close to the house.' And he pointed to the woods. I turned to look at the tree line and shivers went up and down my spine. Hair standing on end, I watched as half a mile away, blue and black lights were streaking through the forest. They were moving so fast that I was having a hard time keeping track of them. These strange phenomenon's and their existence brings us to Jami and her strange and amazing story.

The Legend of Black Lightning at Yok-a-nee continues read at your discretion

A lone figure was running in the darkness dodging tree branches. Jami went out for a jog but was now running for her life. Streaming through the scattered trees in the moon lit night her breath was short. She was frightened to the depths of her soul. Behind her, the woods were ablaze with a strange brilliant blackish ball of crackling light. She glanced over her right shoulder. It was closing in fast. Her moccasin-clad feet carried her swiftly, like a deer, in full gallop. Over the hills, down and across the ridge, she fled with her black hair streaming behind her. On slender, long legs, she glided over stones, around trees, and through creek beds. Straining to see, she suddenly spots something. What is that? In the distance, what is it? No time to stop, she makes one huge, heroic leap and soars, air borne, over the object.

"Oh!" a startled deer bolted in the direction she was running away from. Her ears heard the explosion of electrical activity. She looked back just in time to see the deer engulfed in a crackling ball of lightning. Then, it disappeared into a single dot with a tiny trail of smoke hanging in the cool night air.

"Oh no," she whispered, "faster!" She pushed harder, her heart pounded so loud in her ears but she kept running. After half a mile, she thought surely it was gone. She rotated, running backwards and then stopped. She scanned the woods around her then jogged towards the sound of the cars passing on the highway near the back roads, hoping to hitch a ride home. She was shaking with fright from her and encounter and wanted nothing more than to reach that highway quickly. Just at the edge of the tree line, she saw a brilliant blue and black, jagged flash. Another sparked to her left. She froze. Focusing her vision, she scanned the dark, looking for distortion or any electrical sparks in the black night.

The Legend of Black Lightning at Yok-a-nee continues read at your discretion

Her mind raced. She didn't know if she could run for the freeway or go back the way she came. *No, no, no!* her mind echoed, *never go back, only move forward.* Out of her right eye she saw a tiny blue crackling spark ripple as it struck a pine tree. *You aren't that slick,* she thought.

Jami slowly eased to the ground and groped in the dark for a rock or a stick or anything that she could throw. She found a large tree branch and flung it, crashing twenty or so yards away behind her into the trees. The tree line on both sides of her crackled into brilliant blue black lightning rushing toward the position of the fallen limb. Not just the two that she saw, but also several more balls rushed the limb. She was shocked when she discovered that they had sent an ambush. She counted at least ten or more black, crackling balls racing the same direction.

She dared not move as they raced past her. Se squinted into the darkness and watched as they zigged and zagged deep into the woods behind her. She was surprised that they didn't see her. She touched her shin and felt sweat and mist from the drizzle in the night air. Her skin was cold to the touch and she wondered if her lack of body heat was why they didn't see her. She watched them disappear into the woods.

Jami decided to crawl on her hands and knees out to the highway. She cleared the trees and was sopping wet. Her jogging shorts and bra were soaked and she realized how cold she was. She crossed the guard rail and stuck her thump up in

The Legend of Black Lightning at Yok-a-nee continues read at your discretion

This story is a compilation of Native American folklore about close encounters of the 3rd kind. We refer to as abductions and the 4th kind, Tracking Blood Lines. These close encounters were documented y Native Americans in their tribal legends and storytelling, generating great power for a warrior who had been exposed to a close encounter of the 3rd or 4th kind. He was revered by his Medicine Man and Tribal Chiefs as having connected to the Spirit Walkers and the Creators of the Heavens. He would have great tribal leadership and having his story blended into the tribal legends for generations.

**This page is a compilation of Dead Men Dwarf at Winsor Ruins Internet/Interactive Education series**

The photos on the opposite page are a compilation of the education series of the Legend of Dead Med Dwarf at Winsor Ruins. This series is a breakdown of the author Parker Chamberlain's story elements and is designed to immerse the mind and to educate the reader.

# Folklore Art Characters
## Dead Men Dwarf at Winsor Ruins

The author's detailed story assembly and the elements of the story's complexity and the complexity of Jim Crow politics and its immortal worldwide use in politics. Also the scalable usage to control a population and communities anywhere in the world utilizing its core tools of subjugation, retaliation and many other fear tools to maintain control of ignorance.

# Folklore Art

**Pontatoc**

# Pontatoc Spirit Walker

This native American was captured in the story of the Last Chicksaws and represents how slaves can save an entire community from itself and from outside invaders that have been taken advantage of spiritual beliefs of this tribal group for centuries based on her skill she was able to rescue the tribe from the otherworld visitors of the hive and the nests of the travel chief called Scalpel which proves that the underdog can be the best in times of dare need.

**Folklore Art**
**The Legend of Pali Goddess of Fire**

Which ONE OF You Spoke My Name?

Its Time To Burn Baby Burn!

"Who Was It? Tell ME" Now she Roared! You could Smell •••• the Air Burning all around her, Tiny Sparks were sizzling all over the place;

Milo was Trembling so hard his Teeth were Chattering

Melvin balled up into a Trembling fur Ball!

41

Author Parker Chamberlain created this story title: Pali Goddess of Fire Crocadilla. This compilation is a creature that was featured in the story of Pali Goddess of Fire. His role as a Nimisus of the Great River Hunt with his mate and provides an exciting river hunt scene with Tiger Litty and Beauty Bird of Paradise. Milo Musk Rat and Melvin Bear Cat, two humorous critters create hilarious fun antics through Pali Goddess of Fire in a life and death encounter with these vicious hunters in this funny story. Read Pali Goddess of Fire.

Ophila
War
god

YA KANEE
TRIBE

Moochi

Legend of Black Lighting at Yakanee

The compilation has many Native American tribal players, and Ophelia War Goddess is a lead player in this story and provides the reader with many humorous scenes throughout this funny action packed story written with fun scenes to immerse the mind of the reader in the action of this humorous story authored by Parker Chamberlain. Episodes one through four are wonderful tall tales.

THE TRAVLER

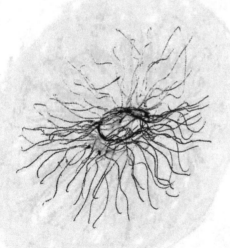

VISITOR

The Traveler: this story written by author Parker Chamberlain in a compilation of close encounters of the 5ᵗʰ kind and immerses the reader's mind into intense mysterious and spine-tingling scenes of nightmarish encounters with an alien visitor that invades the sleep and dreams, creating fear in the lives of the humans they select. This selection is based in blood line and forefathers and mothers whom they track through generations by embedding electronic tracking devices in their nasal cavities from birth to death. These are personal biological property for extrapolating body fluids and in some cases parts and elements that won't be missed.

**Blessed bring righteousness to the world**

# The Last Chickasaw

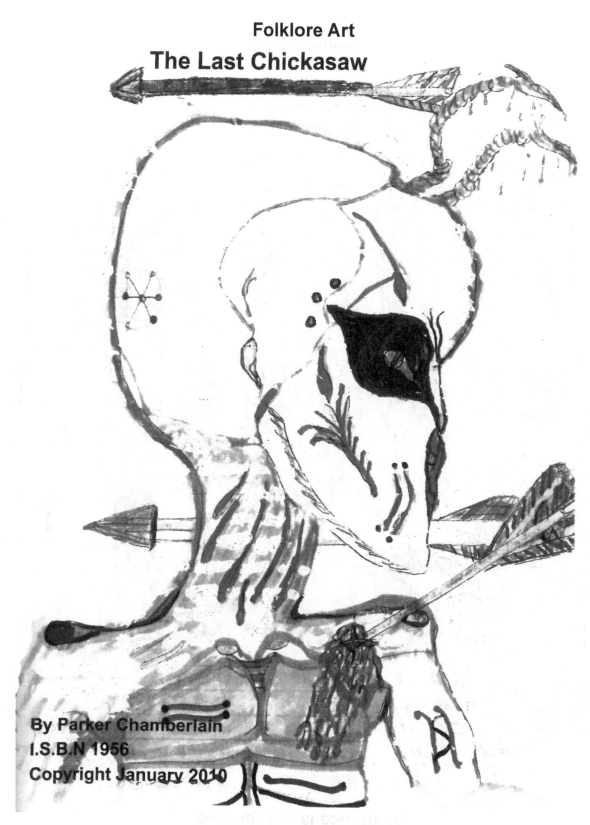

By Parker Chamberlain
I.S.B.N 1956
Copyright January 2010

**Scalpel is deadly**

# Folklore Art

# Vengance

**Vengance is not the end**

# Chapter XXV
## Terrorist Attempt
## At Emerald Mound
## Folklore Art

# EPISODE IV

**A temple of the travelers**

**Inside Masonic Monastery**

**Folklore Art**
**The Blessed Bring Chaos To Order**

**The Gateway Revealed**

# Folklore Art
## Magic Potions

**Folklore Art**

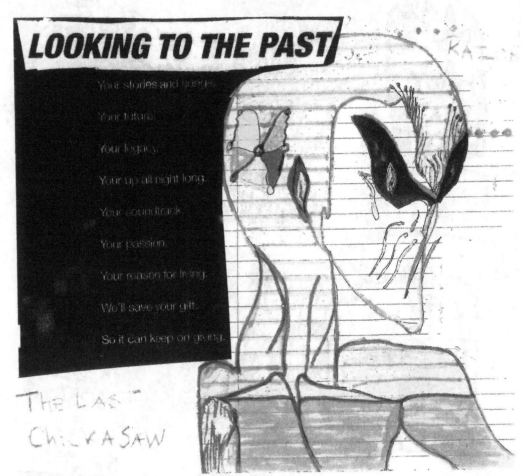

**Razor is dangerous**

# Folklore Art
## Dead Mens Dwarf at Winsor Ruins

# Folklore Art
# SCALAWAGS BROTHERS AND THE EARLY RISERS

Folklore Art
Scalawags Brothers and the
early risers

# Folklore Art
## Rev. Milton Lewis James

The Redd Beastie

**The Redd Beastie**

Folklore Art

# Black Fang

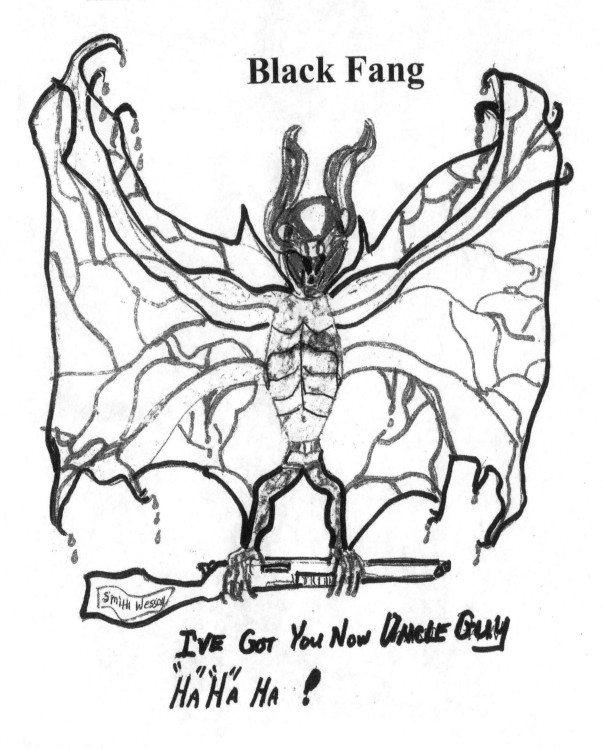

# Folklore Art
## Big Black Winsor Crossing

**The Last Chikasaw**

# Folklore Art
# The Last Chikasaw
# Tribe Pon-ta-toc
# SKIN-U-Alive

# Folklore Art
## Crashed at Roswell 1947

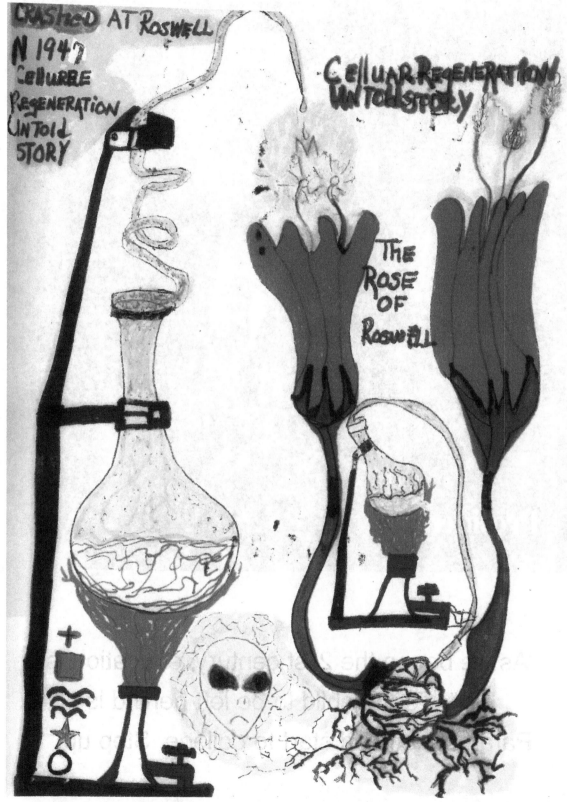

President **Barack Obama**

"As we began the 21st century, education is First. For no child to be left behind is Paramount, head start to college. Step up."

# Internet Interactive
## Dead Mens
## Dwarf at Winsor Ruins

**Product Utility**
**Critical Thinking**
**Knowledge Comprehension**
**Application Analysis Synthesis**
**And EVALUATION.**
**Available At Trafford publishing .com./ Also In E Book**
**Executive Editor\ Education Specialist:  Jamie L. lial**

Grades 4 to 11th

# Internet Interactive
## Student Reader Dead Mens
# Dwarf at Winsor Ruins

**Product Utility**
**Critical Thinking**
**Knowledge Comprehension**
**Application Analysis Synthesis**
**And EVALUATION.**
**Available At Trafford publishing .com./ Also In E Book**
Executive Editor\ Education Specialist:   Jamie L. Hai

**Grades 4 to 11th**

# Student's Internet Interactive Workbook-Dead Men Dwarf at Winsor Ruins

**Hail to the 44th**

Product Utility
Critical Thinking
Knowledge Comprehension
Application Analysis Synthesis
and Evaluation.

Illustrator Parker Chamberlain
Editor/Education Specialist Dr. Jaime L. Lail

# Educational Folklore

**Education Tool**

# The Legend of the

# Aquida

# Nistas

# Of

# Bikini Atoll

**Ms. Bikini and Mr. Atoll**

**Folklore Art from the Story of Pali**

**Goddess of Fire**

**Creepy Consumes Rat**

## Folklore Art

Special Thank You to
Rosa Parks
Civial Rights Activest

Institute for Self Development

Rosa Parks

Civial Rights Activist

1950 2005

Illustrated: 6/1/10
by Parker Chamberlain

## Folklore Art
## Poncho

**Rolling Stones Revenge at Rodney**
**08-14-19**

# CHAPTER XXXII (Our Story Continues)

The Legend
of
Orecal
at
Winsor Ruins

From the Author.

Our sincere thanks to the next pages of contributors to the completion
of this works of art listed and unlisted on the following pages.
To order a list of book, email <u>Dwarfcorp@aol.com</u>

Thank you,
Dwarf Corp Communication

"OUR STORY CONTINUES IN THE LEGEND OF ORECOL AT DEADMEN DWARF AT WINSOR RUINS"

ORDER YOUR COPY AT WWW.TRAFFORD.COM OR email us at DWARFCORP@AOL.COM query book titles. To order Internet query www.traffordbooks.com 1-888-232-4444 or 1-866-941-0370

Author Parker Chamberlain

Illustrator Parker Chamberlain
Executive Editor Jamie L. Lail
Asst. Holly Steck

EXPLORE OUR WEBSITE COMING SOON WWW DEAD MEN DDWARF.COM

Episode 1 order WWW.TRAFFORD.COM
Episode 2
Episode 3

Explore OTHER BOOKS AND E-BOOK BY PARKER CHAMBERLAIN
Bibliography: FOR DEAD MEN DWARF AT WINDSOR RUINS
AS THE AUTHOR I WISH TO EXPRESS MY THANKS TO THE CONTRIBUTOR LISTS BELOW

FOR THERE PHOTOGRAPHS PERIODICALS AND OTHER CONTRIBUTIONS THAT PROVIDED REFERENCE INFORMATION FOR THE COMPLETION OF THESE BOOKS FIRST EDITION, SECOND EDITION, AND THIRD EDITIONS, THANK YOU FROM

PARKER CHAMBERLAIN FOR HELPING ME PROVIDE ELEMENTS TO COMPLETE THESE WORKS OF ART

1. NATIONAL PARKS SERVICE PHOTOGRAPHS OF NATCHEZ TRACE PARKWAY AND PHOTO GALLERY OF HISTORICAL FARMS ALONG THE PARKWAY

2. US DEPARTMENT OF INTERIORS FOR PHOTO GALLERY, FARM HOMES AND BARNS OF AMERICA

3. MISSISSIPPI BATTLE FIELD TOUR PHOTOGRAPHY OF WINDSOR RUINS AND ASSOCIATED PHOTOGRAPHS OF EMERALD MOUND ON THE NATCHEZ TRACE PARKWAY

4. US DEPARTMENT OF INTERIORS FOR PHOTO GALLERY PHOTOGRAPHS OF MOUNT LOCUST AND PHOTOS OF CHURCH STREET IN PORT GIBSON MISSISSIPPI

5. **CATALINA GARCIA** FOR PHOTOGRAPHS OF DWARF TREES AT WINDSOR RUINS

6. **CATALINA GARCIA** FOR PHOTOGRAPHS OF WINDSOR RUINS SIXTEEN COLUMNS

7. MISSISSIPPI BATTLE TOURS PHOTO GALLERY FOR CHURCH STREET PORT GIBSON MISSISSIPPI AND ALL BATTLE FIELD TOUR MARKET SIGNS UTILIZED FOR HISTORICAL VALUE

8. TRAVEL IMAGES.COM FOR PHOTOS OF PHAR MOUNDS FALL HOLLOW FOR FARM PHOTOGRAPHS

9. SHUTTER STOCK.COM FOR FARM PHOTOGRAPHS

10. THE HONORABLE DAVID L GREEN and Juliet Chamberlain Green, STATE REPRESENTATIVE MISSISSIPPI LEGISLATURE FOR FAMILY CONTRIBUTIONS FOR THE COMPLETION OF THIS WORK

11. MISSISSIPPI LEGISLATURE VIA INTERNET INFORMATION THAT PROVIDED HISTORICAL BACKGROUND FOR THIS WORK

12. ALL CORN STATE UNIVERSITY FOR PHOTOGRAPHIC HISTORY OF ITS DEVELOPMENT

13. CITY OF FAYETTE HISTORICAL CONTRIBUTION AND BIRTH PLACE OF THE AUTHOR PARKER CHAMBERLAIN FOR PHOTOGRAPHIC CONTRIBUTIONS

14. CITY OF VICKSBURG FOR PHOTOGRAPHIC CONTRIBUTIONS AT THE HOME OF AUTHOR PARKER CHAMBERLAIN

15. THE STATE OF MISSISSIPPI FOR PHOTOGRAPHIC OPPORTUNITY OF VICKSBURG BATTLE FIELD PHOTOGRAPHS ACQUIRED BY AUTHOR PARKER CHAMBERLAIN

16. TOWN OF LORMAN MISSISSIPPI FOR PHOTOGRAPHIC CONTRIBUTIONS OF LANDSCAPE PHOTOGRAPHS OF ALL CORN STATE UNIVERSITY

17. TOWN OF PORT RODNEY MISSISSIPPI FOR HISTORICAL BACKGROUND OF WINDSOR PLANTATION

18. US DEPARTMENT OF INTERIORS PHOTOS AND BACKGROUND OF PORT RODNEY AND WINDSOR RUINS

19. TOWN OF PORT GIBSON FOR PHOTOS OF CHURCH STREET AND THE FAMOUS PRESBETERIAN CHURCH WITH THE GOLDEN HAND AND ALL THE OTHER HISTORICAL CITY MARKERS THAT CONTRIBUTED TO THIS WORK OF ART

20. PHOTO GALLERY OF PARKER CHAMBERLAIN THAT CONTRIBUTED TO THE COMPLETION OF THIS WORK AND THANKS TO WIKIPEDIA FOR PHOTOS AND DOCUMENTS.

**FROM PARKER CHAMBERLAIN**

THE AUTHOR OF DEAD MENS DWARF AT WINDSOR RUINS, THANK YOU FOR YOUR CONTRIBUTIONS TO THE COMPLETION OF THIS WORK.

"On The Road Home..."

Coffey/Coffie Family Reunion
July 2010 -Fayette /Natchez, Mississippi

The story of West James and Julia coffee James was lived out in this intrepid plantati on house as you look at this picture it is a reminder that our lives and life works are finite, as you look at this picture you don't see the years of barbe Q's, parti es. Planti ng green gardens, picking tomatoes beans corn, okra, hide-n-go seek games we played happy and sad times. Those moments are compressed into our minds, the grand children of this couple. My grand children will only see this broken down rusting weathered hulk of a house in this book because ti me has erased this home but the families that were born in this home are flourishing and scattered around America, Milton L. James and Shelly James. and Hester James Chamberlain are the down line slave descendants of the this family, that has produced Teachers, Doctors Lawyers, Dentist, politicians, and many others, because of REAL TREASURE, EDUCATION, OUR PARENTS, STEPPED UP, AND REMINDED THEIR CHILDREN, NEVER FORGET JIM CROW IS IMMORTAL, AND PREYS ON IGNORANCE.

# CD's and Sound track of Folklore Music
# Dwarfcorp Dallas

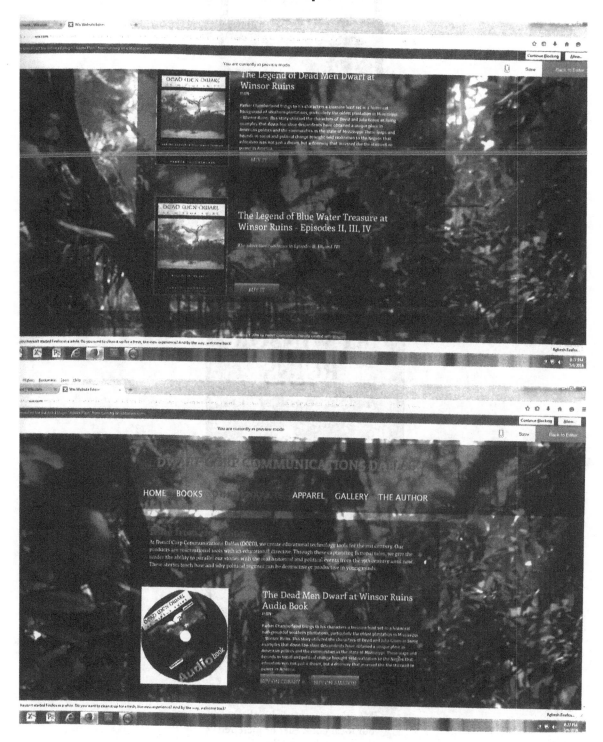

# THE LEGEND OF DEAD MEN DWARF AT WINSOR RUINS

And the legend of Blue Water Treasure

EPISODE I

by
PARKER CHAMBERLAIN

Available now from
Trafford Publishing
www.trafford.com

This title is also available through
your local bookseller or preferred
on-line retailer.

**Folklore Art**

**Educational tool to increase knowledge**

# TEA

## Texas Education Agency
## Student Assessment Directory

## For Home Study Links Call (512)-463-9536

NOTE: The English and Spanish versions of STAAR assess the same reporting categories and TEKS standards.

**STAAR TEKS LINKS available at this number**

**Students - Parents - Teachers**

Utilize this links to increase children's learning capability. This link will provide additional testing tools for better test grades.

**(512)-463-9536**

## FRIENDS of the Library

To the Executive librarian, this is a gift to the library from Parker Chamberlain, author of "Dead Men Dwarf at Winsor Ruins," Episodes I, II, III, IV, a series of short stories written about my childhood, growing up in Mississippi during the late fifties and transitional 60s. I wish you to display this gift and add it to your card catalog. So many others who have a great story may enjoy the rich history of my life, mix with a little Mark Twain's humor and a bit of Edgar Allan Poe's darkness.

Your library will receive Future Productions. The next issues of "The Last Chickasaw" is in Production Episode I, II, III, IV, V, VI.

Please use the web page attached to get more stories by Author Parker Chamberlain at TraffordPublishing.com bookstore
ISBN – 10:1466 945 923/Hard copies/Soft copies/E-book

| | |
|---|---|
| Also: Ava – Audio Book | At DwarfCorp@aol.com |
| On Request: - MP3 | Email request, special order |
| CDs | to Audio Book. |
| | Include your email, return |
| | address and phone. |

**Happy Reading**

Thank You,
Parker Chamberlain, Author CEO
Dwarf Corp. Creative Authors

Parker Chamberlain was born during the late 50's in Fayette, Mississippi, during a time when Jim Crow was the most dangerous criminal in America, Parker Chamberlain is a, native of Vicksburg, Mississippi. He like most American witnessed the Vietnam war, the political destruction and assassination of John F Kennedy and Bobby Kennedy and the assassination of Dr. Martin Luther King, and hundreds of individual micro cosms of change, all across America, birth pains of change, political war, water gate. Iran kuntra scandal, the moon landing. Ten presidents elected and the most surprising event in American history, the 44th president elected to office Barack Obama, the first black American president, proof positive that education and political activeness and a life death struggle with Jim Crow politics, changed the civil rights and political face of a nation. At her best, stars and stripes waiving in the winds and her worst, fire hoses blasting people in the streets in Selma, Alabama in the 60s, witnessing these events, will make Parker Chamberlain a great author through the 21st century.

The social and political change that began with the emancipation proclamation from the 1800's thru the 1900's, brought political change and self realization to the Negro's, that education was not just a dream, but a doorway that accessed the stair well to power in America; a clear message Unlocked by President Kennedy in the 1963 and 1964 Voting Rights Act, to young Black Americans that a turning point has been achieved. It began with 40 acres and a mule and has climaxed at the 44th president, a Black American; Barrack-O-bama, proof positive that America has reached her turning point. Envoked by Dr. Martin Luther King I Have a dream, America has more work ahead. Parker Chamberlain has spun a beautiful story of the Achievement of the American Experience not a Fiction, but a true story of his families American experience. Touch by the divine the Real Hunt For Treasure is Education, Political Activeness in The Communities of Our America.

Dead Men Dwarf at Windsor Ruins Teachers Key

Internet Group Activities: Research, other burial mound. Discuss the purpose designs throughout the world includes the Great Pyramid of Egypt.

Collect: Five-page essay about these burial system, grade on contents, details, contents, assembly and comprehension.

The research continues: Trafford.com for more of the author Parker Chamberlain

Disclaimer: Parker Chamberlain

As with all education products, the author created this product as a training system for simple assessment of reading, writing entertainment, its educational values is ascertained by the user of this product.

Illustration: Parker Chamberlain
Copyright: Parker Chamberlain
Copyright date: January 2012
All rights reserved: Parker Chamberlain and Catalina Cantu Garcia

Printed in the United States
By Bookmasters